D1522588

Collected Stories

Charlotte Riddell

IndoEuropean
Publishing.com
Los Angeles, CA, USA

CONTENTS

The Open Door 1

The Old House in Vauxhall Walk 43

The Last of Squire Ennismore 66

THE OPEN DOOR

Some people do not believe in ghosts. For that matter, some people do not believe in anything.

There are persons who even affect incredulity concerning that open door at Ladlow Hall. They say it did not stand wide open—that they could have shut it; that the whole affair was a delusion; that they are sure it must have been a conspiracy; that they are doubtful whether there is such a place as Ladlow on the face of the earth; that the first time they are in Meadowshire they will look it up.

That is the manner in which this story, hitherto unpublished, has been greeted by my acquaintances. How it will be received by strangers is quite another matter. I am going to tell what happened to me exactly as it happened, and readers can credit or scoff at the tale as it pleases them. It is not necessary for me to find faith and comprehension in addition to a ghost story, for the world at large. If such were the case, I should lay down my pen.

Perhaps, before going further, I ought to premise there was a time when I did not believe in ghosts either. If you had asked me one summer's morning years ago when you met me on London Bridge if I held such appearances to be probable or possible, you would have received an emphatic 'No' for answer.

But, at this rate, the story of the Open Door will never be told; so we will, with your permission, plunge into it immediately.

'Sandy!'

'What do you want?'

'Should you like to earn a sovereign?'

'Of course I should.'

A somewhat curt dialogue, but we were given to curtness in the office of Messrs Frimpton, Frampton and Fryer, auctioneers and estate agents, St Benet's Hill, City.

(My name is not Sandy or anything like it, but the other clerks so styled me because of a real or fancied likeness to some character, an ill-looking Scotchman, they had seen at the theatre. From this it may be inferred I was not handsome. Far from it. The only ugly specimen in my family, I knew I was very plain; and it chanced to be no secret to me either that I felt grievously discontented with my lot. I did not like the occupation of clerk in an auctioneer's office, and I did not like my employers.

We are all of us inconsistent, I suppose, for it was a shock to me to find they entertained a most cordial antipathy to me.)

'Because,' went on Parton, a fellow, my senior by many years—a fellow who delighted in chaffing me, 'I can tell you how to lay hands on one.'

'How?' I asked, sulkily enough, for I felt he was having what he called his fun.

'You know that place we let to Carrison, the tea-dealer?' Carrison was a merchant in the China trade, possessed of fleets of vessels and towns of warehouses; but I did not correct Parton's expression, I simply nodded.

'He took it on a long lease, and he can't live in it; and our governor said this morning he wouldn't mind giving anybody who could

2

find out what the deuce is the matter, a couple of sovereigns and his travelling expenses.'

'Where is the place?' I asked, without turning my head; for the convenience of listening I had put my elbows on the desk and propped up my face with both hands.

'Away down in Meadowshire, in the heart of the grazing country.'

'And what is the matter?' I further enquired.

'A door that won't keep shut.'

'What?'

'A door that will keep open, if you prefer that way of putting it,' said Parton.

'You are jesting.'

'If I am, Carrison is not, or Fryer either. Carrison came here in a nice passion, and Fryer was in a fine rage; I could see he was, though he kept his temper outwardly. They have had an active correspondence it appears, and Carrison went away to talk to his lawyer. Won't make much by that move, I fancy.'

'But tell me,' I entreated, 'why the door won't keep shut?'

'They say the place is haunted.'

'What nonsense!' I exclaimed.

Then you are just the person to take the ghost in hand. I thought so while old Fryer was speaking.'

3

'If the door won't keep shut,' I remarked, pursuing my own train of thought, 'why can't they let it stay open?'

'I have not the slightest idea. I only know there are two sovereigns to be made, and that I give you a present of the information.'

And having thus spoken, Parton took down his hat and went out, either upon his own business or that of his employers.

There was one thing I can truly say about our office, we were never serious in it. I fancy that is the case in most offices nowadays; at all events, it was the case in ours. We were always chaffing each other, playing practical jokes, telling stupid stories, scamping our work, looking at the clock, counting the weeks to next St Lubbock's Day, counting the hours to Saturday.

For all that we were all very earnest in our desire to have our salaries raised, and unanimous in the opinion no fellows ever before received such wretched pay. I had twenty pounds a year, which I was aware did not half provide for what I ate at home. My mother and sisters left me in no doubt on the point, and when new clothes were wanted I always hated to mention the fact to my poor worried father.

We had been better off once, I believe, though I never remember the time. My father owned a small property in the country, but owing to the failure of some bank, I never could understand what bank, it had to be mortgaged; then the interest was not paid, and the mortgages foreclosed, and we had nothing left save the half-pay of a major, and about a hundred a year which my mother brought to the common fund.

We might have managed on our income, I think, if we had not been so painfully genteel; but we were always trying to do something quite beyond our means, and consequently debts accumulated, and creditors ruled us with rods of iron.

Before the final smash came, one of my sisters married the younger son of a distinguished family, and even if they had been disposed to live comfortably and sensibly she would have kept her sisters up to the mark. My only brother, too, was an officer, and of course the family thought it necessary he should see we preserved appearances.

It was all a great trial to my father, I think, who had to bear the brunt of the dunning and harass, and eternal shortness of money; and it would have driven me crazy if I had not found a happy refuge when matters were going wrong at home at my aunt's. She was my father's sister, and had married so 'dreadfully below her' that my mother refused to acknowledge the relationship at all.

For these reasons and others, Parton's careless words about the two sovereigns stayed in my memory.

I wanted money badly—I may say I never had sixpence in the world of my own—and I thought if I could earn two sovereigns I might buy some trifles I needed for myself, and present my father with a new umbrella. Fancy is a dangerous little jade to flirt with, as I soon discovered.

She led me on and on. First I thought of the two sovereigns; then I recalled the amount of the rent Mr Carrison agreed to pay for Ladlow Hall; then I decided he would gladly give more than two sovereigns if he could only have the ghost turned out of possession. I fancied I might get ten pounds—twenty pounds. I considered the matter all day, and I dreamed of it all night, and when I dressed myself next morning I was determined to speak to Mr Fryer on the subject.

I did so—I told that gentleman Parton had mentioned the matter to me, and that if Mr Fryer had no objection, I should like to try whether I could not solve the mystery. I told him I had been accustomed to lonely houses, and that I should not feel at all

5

nervous; that I did not believe in ghosts, and as for burglars, I was not afraid of them.

'I don't mind your trying,' he said at last. 'Of course you understand it is no cure, no pay. Stay in the house for a week; if at the end of that time you can keep the door shut, locked, bolted, or nailed up, telegraph for mc, and I will go down—if not, come back. If you like to take a companion there is no objection.'

I thanked him, but said I would rather not have a companion.

'There is only one thing, sir, I should like,' I ventured.

'And that—?' he interrupted.

'Is a little more money. If I lay the ghost, or find out the ghost, I think I ought to have more than two sovereigns.'

'How much more do you think you ought to have?' he asked.

His tone quite threw me off my guard, it was so civil and conciliatory, and I answered boldly:

'Well, if Mr Carrison cannot now live in the place perhaps he wouldn't mind giving me a ten-pound note.'

Mr Fryer turned, and opened one of the books lying on his desk. He did not look at or refer to it in any war—I saw that.

'You have been with us how long, Edlyd?' he said.

'Eleven months tomorrow,' I replied.

'And our arrangement was, I think, quarterly payments, and one month's notice on either side?'

'Yes, sir.' I heard my voice tremble, though I could not have said what frightened me.

'Then you will please to take your notice now. Come in before you leave this evening, and I'll pay you three months' salary, and then we shall be quits.'

'I don't think I quite understand,' I was beginning, when he broke in:

'But I understand, and that's enough. I have had enough of you and your airs, and your indifference, and your insolence here. I never had a clerk I disliked as I do you. Coming and dictating terms, forsooth! No, you shan't go to Ladlow. Many a poor chap'—(he said 'devil')—- 'would have been glad to earn half a guinea, let alone two sovereigns; and perhaps you may be before you are much older.'

'Do you mean that you won't keep me here any longer, sir?' I asked in despair. I had no intention of offending you. I—'

'Now you need not say another word,' he interrupted, 'for I won't bandy words with you.

Since you have been in this place you have never known your position, and you don't seem able to realize it. When I was foolish enough to take you, I did it on the strength of your connections, but your connections have done nothing for mc. I have never had a penny out of any one of your friends—if you have any. You'll not do any good in business for yourself or anybody else, and the sooner you go to Australia'—(here he was very emphatic)—and get off these premises, the better I shall be pleased.'

I did not answer him—I could not. He had worked himself to a white heat by this time, and evidently intended I should leave his premises then and there. He counted five pounds out of his cashbox, and, writing a receipt, pushed it and the money across the table, and bade me sign and be off at once.

My hand trembled So I could scarcely hold the pen, but I had presence of mind enough left to return one pound ten in gold, and three shillings and fourpence I had, quite by the merest good fortune, in my waistcoat pocket.

'I can't take wages for work I haven't done,' I said, as well as sorrow and passion would let me. 'Good-morning,' and I left his office and passed out among the clerks.

I took from my desk the few articles belonging to me, left the papers it contained in order, and then, locking it, asked Parton if he would be so good as to give the key to Mr Fryer.

'What's up?' he asked 'Are you going?'

I said, 'Yes, I am going'.

'Got the sack?'

'That is exactly what has happened.'

'Well, I'm—!' exclaimed Mr Parton.

I did not stop to hear any further commentary on the matter, but bidding my fellow-clerks goodbye, shook the dust of Frimpton's Estate and Agency Office from off my feet.

I did not like to go home and say I was discharged, so I walked about aimlessly, and at length found myself in Regent Street. There I met my father, looking more worried than usual.

'Do you think, Phil,' he said (my name is Theophilus), 'you could get two or three pounds from your employers?'

Maintaining a discreet silence regarding what had passed, I answered:

'No doubt I could.'

I shall be glad if you will then, my boy,' he went on, for we are badly in want of it.'

I did not ask him what was the special trouble. Where would have been the use? There was always something—gas, or water, or poor-rates, or the butcher, or the baker, or the bootmaker.

Well, it did not much matter, for we were well accustomed to the life; but, I thought, 'if ever I marry, we will keep within our means'. And then there rose up before me a vision of Patty, my cousin—the blithest, prettiest, most useful, most sensible girl that ever made sunshine in poor man's house.

My father and I had parted by this time, and I was still walking aimlessly on, when all at once an idea occurred to me. Mr Fryer had not treated me well or fairly. I would hoist him on his own petard. I would go to headquarters, and try to make terms with Mr Carrison direct.

No sooner thought than done. I hailed a passing omnibus, and was ere long in the heart of the city. Like other great men, Mr Carrison was difficult of access—indeed, so difficult of access, that the clerk to whom I applied for an audience told me plainly I could not see him at all. I might send in my message if I liked, he was good enough to add, and no doubt it would be attended to. I said I should not send in a message, and was then asked what I would do. My answer was simple. I meant to wait till I did see him. I was told they could not have people waiting about the office in this way.

I said I supposed I might stay in the street. 'Carrison didn't own that,' I suggested.

The clerk advised me not to try that game, or I might get locked up.

I said I would take my chance of it.

After that we went on arguing the question at some length, and we were in the middle of a heated argument, in which several of Carrison's 'young gentlemen', as they called themselves, were good enough to join, when we were all suddenly silenced by a grave-looking individual, who authoritatively enquired:

'What is all this noise about?'

Before anyone could answer I spoke up:

'I want to see Mr Carrison, and they won't let me.'

'What do you want with Mr Garrison?'

'I will tell that to himself only.'

'Very well, say on—I am Mr Garrison.'

For a moment I felt abashed and almost ashamed of my persistency; next instant, however, what Mr Fryer would have called my 'native audacity' came to the rescue, and I said, drawing a step or two nearer to him, and taking off my hat:

'I wanted to speak to you about Ladlow hall, if you please, sir.'

In an instant the fashion of his face changed, a look of irritation succeeded to that of immobility; an angry contraction of the eyebrows disfigured the expression of his countenance.

'Ladlow Hall!' he repeated; 'and what have you got to say about Ladlow Hall?'

'That is what I wanted to tell you, sir,' I answered, and a dead hush seemed to fall on the office as I spoke.

The silence seemed to attract his attention, for he looked sternly at the clerks, who were not using a pen or moving a finger.

'Come this way, then,' he said abruptly; and next minute I was in his private office.

'Now, what is it?' he asked, flinging himself into a chair, and addressing me, who stood hat in hand beside the great table in the middle of the room.

I began—I will say he was a patient listener—at the very beginning, and told my story straight trough. I concealed nothing. I enlarged on nothing. A discharged clerk I stood before him, and in the capacity of a discharged clerk I said what I had to say. He heard me to the end, then he sat silent, thinking.

At last he spoke.

'You have heard a great deal of conversation about Ladlow, I suppose?' he remarked.

'No sir; I have heard nothing except what I have told you.'

'And why do you desire to strive to solve such a mystery?'

'If there is any money to be made, I should like to make it, sir.'

'How old are you?'

'Two-and-twenty last January.'

'And how much salary had you at Frimpton's?'

11

'Twenty pounds a year.'

'Humph! More than you are worth, I should say.'

'Mr Fryer seemed to imagine so, sir, at any rate,' I agreed, sorrowfully.

'But what do you think?' he asked, smiling in spite of himself.

'I think I did quite as much work as the other clerks,' I answered.

'That is not saying much, perhaps,' he observed. I was of his opinion, but I held my peace.

'You will never make much of a clerk, I am afraid,' Mr Garrison proceeded, fitting his disparaging remarks upon me as he might on a lay figure. 'You don't like desk work?'

'Not much, sir.'

'I should judge the best thing you could do would be to emigrate,' he went on, eyeing me critically.

'Mr Fryer said I had better go to Australia or—' I stopped, remembering the alternative that gentleman had presented.

'Or where?' asked Mr Carrison.

'The—-, sir' I explained, softly and apologetically.

He laughed—he lay back in his chair and laughed—and I laughed myself, though ruefully.

After all, twenty pounds was twenty pounds, though I had not thought much of the salary till I lost it.

We went on talking for a long time after that; he asked me all about my father and my early life, and how we lived, and where we lived, and the people we knew; and, in fact, put more questions than I can well remember.

'It seems a crazy thing to do,' he said at last; 'and yet I feel disposed to trust you. The house is standing perfectly empty. I can't live in it, and I can't get rid of it; all my own furniture I have removed, and there is nothing in the place except a few old-fashioned articles belonging to Lord Ladlow. The place is a loss to me. It is of no use trying to let it, and thus, in fact, matters are at a deadlock. You won't be able to find out anything, I know, because, of course, others have tried to solve the mystery ere now; still, if you like to try you may. I will make this bargain with you.

If you like to go down, I will pay your reasonable expenses for a fortnight; and if you do any good for mc, I will give you a ten-pound note for yourself. Of course I must be satisfied that what you have told me is true and tat you are what you represent. Do you know anybody in the city who would speak for you?'

I could think of no one but my uncle. I hinted to Mr Carrison he was not grand enough or rich enough, perhaps, but I knew nobody else to whom I could refer him.

'What!' he said, 'Robert Dorland, of Cullum Street. He does business with us. If he will go bail for your good behaviour I shan't want any further guarantee. Come along.' And to my intense amazement, he rose, put on his hat, walked me across the outer office and along the pavements till we came to Cullum Street.

'Do you know this youth, Mr Dorland?' he said, standing in front of my uncle's desk, and laying a hand on my shoulder.

'Of course I do, Mr Carrison,' answered my uncle, a little apprehensively; for, as he told me afterwards, he could not imagine what mischief I had been up to. 'He is my nephew.'

'And what is your opinion of him—do you think he is a young fellow I may safely trust?'

My uncle smiled, and answered, 'That depends on what you wish to trust him with.'

'A long column of addition, for instance.'

'It would be safer to give that task to somebody else.'

'Oh, uncle!' I remonstrated; for I had really striven to conquer my natural antipathy to figures—worked hard, and every bit of it against the collar.

My uncle got off his stool, and said, standing with his back to the empty fire-grate: 'Tell me what you wish the boy to do, Mr Carrison, and I will tell you whether he will suit your purpose or not. I know him, I believe, better than he knows himself.'

In an easy, affable way, for so rich a man, Mr Carrison took possession of the vacant stool, and nursing his right leg over his left knee, answered:

'He wants to go and shut the open door at Ladlow for mc. Do you think he can do that?'

My uncle looked steadily back at the speaker, and said, 'I thought, Mr Carrison, it was quite settled no one could shut it?'

Mr Carrison shifted a little uneasily on his scat, and replied: I did not set your nephew the task he fancies he would like to undertake.'

'Have nothing to do with it, Phil,' advised my uncle, shortly.

'You don't believe in ghosts, do you, Mr Dorland?' asked Mr Carrison, with a slight sneer.

'Don't you, Mr Carrison?' retorted my uncle.

There was a pause—an uncomfortable pause—during the course of which I felt the ten pounds, which, in imagination, I had really spent, trembling in the scale. I was not afraid. For ten pounds, or half the money, I would have faced all the inhabitants of spirit land. I longed to tell them so; but something in the way those two men looked at each other stayed my tongue.

'If you ask me the question here in the heart of the city, Mr Dorland,' said Mr Carrison, at length, slowly and carefully, 'I answer "No"; but it you were to put it to me on a dark night at Ladlow, I should beg time to consider. I do not believe in supernatural phenomena myself, and yet—the door at Ladlow is as much beyond my comprehension as the ebbing and flowing of the sea.'

'And you can't Live at Ladlow?' remarked my uncle.

'I can't live at Ladlow, and what is more, I can't get anyone else to live at Ladlow.'

'And you want to get rid of your lease?'

'I want so much to get rid of my lease that I told Fryer I would give him a handsome sum if he could induce anyone to solve the mystery. Is there any other information you desire, Mr Dorland? Because if here is, you have only to ask and have. I feel I am not here in a prosaic office in the city of London, but in the Palace of Truth.'

My uncle took no notice of the implied compliment. When wine is good it needs no bush. If a man is habitually honest

15

in his speech and in his thoughts, he desires no recognition of the fact.

'I don't think so,' he answered; 'it is for the boy to say what he will do. If he be advised by me he will stick to his ordinary work in his employers' office, and leave ghost-hunting and spirit-laying alone.'

Mr Carrison shot a rapid glance in my direction, a glance which, implying a secret understanding, might have influenced my uncle could I have stooped to deceive my uncle.

'I can't stick to my work there any longer,' I said. 'I got my marching orders today.'

'What had you been doing, Phil?' asked my uncle.

'I wanted ten pounds to go and lay the ghost!' I answered, so dejectedly, that both Mr Carrison and my uncle broke out laughing.

'Ten pounds!' cried my uncle, almost between laughing and crying. 'Why, Phil boy, I had rather, poor man though I am, have given thee ten pounds than that thou should'st go ghost-hunting or ghostlaying.'

When he was very much in earnest my uncle went back to thee and thou of his native dialect. I liked the vulgarism, as my mother called it, and I knew my aunt loved to hear him use the caressing words to her. He had risen, not quite from the ranks it is true, but if ever a gentleman came ready born into the world it was Robert Dorland, upon whom at our home everyone seemed to look down.

'What will you do, Edlyd?' asked Mr Carrison; 'you hear what your uncle says, "Give up the enterprise," and what I say; I do not want either to bribe or force your inclinations.'

'I will go, sir,' I answered quite steadily. I am not afraid, and I should like to show you—' I stopped. I had been going to say, 'I should like to show you I am not such a fool as you all take me for', but I felt such an address would be too familiar, and refrained.

Mr Carrison looked at me curiously. I think he supplied the end of the sentence for himself, but he only answered:

'I should like you to show me that door fast shut; at any rate, if you can stay in the place alone for a fortnight, you shall have your money.'

'I don't like it, Phil,' said my uncle: 'I don't like this freak at all.'

'I am sorry for that, uncle,' I answered, 'for I mean to go.

'When?' asked Mr Carrison.

'Tomorrow morning,' I replied.

'Give him five pounds, Dorland, please, and I will send you my cheque. You will account to me for that sum, you understand,' added Mr Garrison, turning to where I stood.

'A sovereign will be quite enough,' I said.

'You will take five pounds, and account to me for it,' repeated Mr Carrison, firmly; 'also, you will write to me every day, to my private address, and if at any moment you feel the thing too much for you, throw it up. Good afternoon,' and without more formal leavetaking he departed.

'It is of no use talking to you, Phil, I suppose?' said my uncle.

'I don't think it is,' I replied; 'you won't say anything to them at home, will you?'

'I am not very likely to meet any of them, am I?' he answered, without a shade of bitterness—-merely stating a fact.

'I suppose I shall not see you again before I start,' I said, 'so I will bid you goodbye now.

'Goodbye, my lad; I wish I could see you a bit wiser and steadier.'

I did not answer him; my heart was very full, and my eyes too. I had tried, but office-work was not in me, and I felt it was just as vain to ask me to sit on a stool and pore over writing and figures as to think a person born destitute of musical ability could compose an opera.

Of course I went straight to Patty; though we were not then married, though sometimes it seemed to me as if we never should be married, she was my better half then as she is my better half now.

She did not throw cold water on the project; she did not discourage me. What she said, with her dear face aglow with excitement, was, 'I only wish, Phil, I was going with you.' Heaven knows, so did I.

Next morning I was up before the milkman. I had told my people overnight I should be going out of town on business. Patty and I settled the whole plan in detail. I was to breakfast and dress there, for I meant to go down to Ladlow in my volunteer garments. That was a subject upon which my poor father and I never could agree; he called volunteering child's play, and other things equally hard to bear; whilst my brother, a very carpet warrior to my mind, was never weary of ridiculing the force, and chaffing me for imagining I was 'a soldier'.

Patty and I had talked matters over, and settled, as I have said, that I should dress at her father's.

A young fellow I knew had won a revolver at a raffle, and willingly lent it to me. With that and my rifle I felt I could conquer an army.

It was a lovely afternoon when I found myself walking through leafy lanes in the heart of Meadowshire. With every vein of my heart I loved the country, and the country was looking its best just then: grass ripe for the mower, grain forming in the ear, rippling streams, dreamy rivers, old orchards, quaint cottages.

'Oh that I had never to go back to London,' I thought, for I am one of the few people left on earth who love the country and hate cities. I walked on, I walked a long way, and being uncertain as to my road, asked a gentleman who was slowly riding a powerful roan horse under arching trees—a gentleman accompanied by a young lady mounted on a stiff white pony—my way to Ladlow Hall.

'That is Ladlow Hall,' he answered, pointing with his whip over the fence to my left hand. I thanked him and was going on, when he said:

'No one is living there now.'

'I am aware of that,' I answered.

He did not say anything more, only courteously bade me good-day, and rode off. The young lady inclined her head in acknowledgement of my uplifted cap, and smiled kindly. Altogether I felt pleased, little things always did please me. It was a good beginning—half-way to a good ending!

When I got to the Lodge I showed Mr Garrison's letter to the woman, and received the key.

'You are not going to stop up at the Hall alone, are you, sir?' she asked.

'Yes, I am,' I answered, uncompromisingly, so uncompromisingly that she said no more.

The avenue led straight to the house; it was uphill all the way, and bordered by rows of the most magnificent limes I ever beheld. A light iron fence divided the avenue from the park, and between the trunks of the trees I could see the deer browsing and cattle grazing. Ever and anon there came likewise to my ear the sound of a sheep-bell.

It was a long avenue, but at length I stood in front of the Hall—a square, solid-looking, old-fashioned house, three stories high, with no basement; a flight of steps up to the principal entrance; four windows to the right of the door, four windows to the left; the whole building flanked and backed with trees; all the blinds pulled down, a dead silence brooding over the place: the sun westering behind the great trees studding the park. I took all this in as I approached, and afterwards as I stood for a moment under the ample porch; then, remembering the business which had brought me so far, I fitted the great key in the lock, turned the handle, and entered Ladlow Hall.

For a minute—stepping out of the bright sunlight—the place looked to me so dark that I could scarcely distinguish the objects by which I was surrounded; but my eyes soon grew accustomed to the comparative darkness, and I found I was in an immense hall, lighted from the roof, a magnificent old oak staircase conducted to the upper rooms.

The floor was of black and white marble. There were two fireplaces, fitted with dogs for burning wood; around the walls hung pictures, antlers, and horns, and in odd niches and corners stood groups of statues, and the figures of men in complete suits of armour.

To look at the place outside, no one would have expected to find such a hall. I stood lost in amazement and admiration, and then I began to glance more particularly around.

Mr Garrison had not given me any instructions by which to identify the ghostly chamber—-which I concluded would most probably be found on the first floor.

I knew nothing of the story connected with it—if there were a story. On that point I had left London as badly provided with mental as with actual luggage—worse provided, indeed, for a hamper, packed by Patty, and a small bag were coming over from the station; but regarding the mystery I was perfectly unencumbered. I had not the faintest idea in which apartment it resided.

Well, I should discover that, no doubt, for myself ere long.

I looked around me—doors—doors—doors I had never before seen so many doors together all at once. Two of them stood open—one wide, the other slightly ajar.

'I'll just shut them as a beginning,' I thought, 'before I go upstairs.'

The doors were of oak, heavy, well-fitting, furnished with good locks and sound handles. After I had closed I tried them. Yes, they were quite secure. I ascended the great staircase feeling curiously like an intruder, paced the corridors, entered the many bed-chambers—some quite bare of furniture, others containing articles of an ancient fashion, and no doubt of considerable value—chairs, antique dressing- tables, curious wardrobes, and such like. For the most part the doors were closed, and I shut those that stood open before making my way into the attics.

I was greatly delighted with the attics. The windows lighting them did not, as a rule, overlook the front of the Hall, but commanded wide views over wood, and valley, and meadow. Leaning out of one, I could see, that to the right of the Hall the ground, thickly planted, shelved down to a stream, which came out into the daylight a little distance beyond the plantation, and meandered through the deer park. At the back of the Hall the windows looked out on nothing save a dense wood and a portion of the stable-yard, whilst on the side nearest the point from whence I had come there were spreading gardens surrounded by thick yew hedges, and kitchen-gardens protected by high walls; and further on a farmyard, where I could perceive cows and oxen, and, further still, luxuriant meadows, and fields glad with waving corn.

'What a beautiful place!' I said. 'Garrison must have been a duffer to leave it.' And then I thought what a great ramshackle house it was for anyone to be in all alone.

Getting heated with my long walk, I suppose, made me feel chilly, for I shivered as I drew my head in from the last dormer window, and prepared to go downstairs again.

In the attics, as in the other parts of the house I had as yet explored, I closed the doors, when there were keys locking them; when there were not, trying them, and in all cases, leaving them securely fastened.

When I reached the ground floor the evening was drawing on apace, and I felt that if I wanted to explore the whole house before dusk I must hurry my proceedings.

'I'll take the kitchens next,' I decided, and so made my way to a wilderness of domestic offices lying to the rear of the great hall. Stone passages, great kitchens, an immense servants'-hall, larders, pantries, coal-cellars, beer-cellars, laundries, brewhouses, housekeeper's room—it was not of any use lingering over these details. The mystery that troubled Mr Garrison could scarcely lodge amongst cinders and empty bottles, and there did not seem much else left in this part of the building.

I would go through the living-rooms, and then decide as to the apartments I should occupy myself.

The evening shadows were drawing on apace, so I hurried back into the hall, feeling it was a weird position to be there all alone with those ghostly hollow figures of men in armour, and the statues on which the moon's beams must fall so coldly. I would just look through the lower apartments and then kindle a fire. I had seen quantities of wood in a cupboard close at hand, and felt that beside a blazing hearth, and after a good cup of tea, I should not feel the solitary sensation which was oppressing me.

The sun had sunk below the horizon by this time, for to reach Ladlow I had been obliged to travel by cross lines of railway, and wait besides for such trains as condescended to carry third-class passengers; but there was still light enough in the hail to see all objects distinctly. With my own eyes I saw that one of the doors I had shut with my own hands was standing wide!

I turned to the door on the other side of the hail. It was as I had left it—closed. This, then, was the room—this with the open door For a second I stood appalled; I think I was fairly frightened.

That did not last long, however. There lay the work I had desired to undertake, the foe I had offered to fight; so without more ado I shut the door and tried it.

'Now I will walk to the end of the hall and sec what happens,' I considered. I did so. I walked to the foot of the grand staircase and back again, and looked.

The door stood wide open.

I went into the room, after just a spasm of irresolution—went in and pulled up the blinds: a good-sized room, twenty by twenty (I knew, because I paced it afterwards), lighted by two long windows.

The floor, of polished oak, was partially covered with a Turkey carpet. There were two recesses beside the fireplace, one fitted up as a bookcase, the other with an old and elaborately caned cabinet. I was astonished also to find a bedstead in an apartment so little retired from the traffic of the house; and there were also some chairs of an obsolete make, covered, so far as I could make out, with Faded tapestry. Beside the bedstead, which stood against the wall opposite to the door, I perceived another door. It was fast locked, the only locked door I had as yet met with in the interior of the house. It was a dreary, gloomy room: the dark panelled walls; the black, shining floor; the windows high from the ground; the antique furniture; the dull four-poster bedstead, with dingy velvet curtains; the gaping chimney; the silk counterpane that looked like a pall.

'Any crime might have been committed in such a room,' I thought pettishly; and then I looked at the door critically.

Someone had been at the trouble of fitting bolts upon it, for when I passed out I not merely shut the door securely, but bolted it as well.

'I will go and get some wood, and then look at it again,' I soliloquized. When I came back it stood wide open once more.

'Stay open, then!' I cried in a fury. 'I won't trouble myself any more with you tonight!'

Almost as I spoke the words, there came a ring at the front door. Echoing through the desolate house, the peal in the then state of my nerves startled me beyond expression.

It was only the man who had agreed to bring over my traps. I bade him lay them down in the ball, and, while looking out some small silver, asked where the nearest post-office was to be found. Not far from the park gates, he said; if I wanted any letter sent, he would drop it in the box for me; the mail-cart picked up the bag at ten o'clock.

I had nothing ready to post then, and told him so. Perhaps the money I gave was more than he expected, or perhaps the dreariness of my position impressed him as it had impressed mc, for he paused with his hand on the lock, and asked:

'Are you going to stop here all alone, master?'

'All alone,' I answercd, with such cheerfulness as was possible under the circumstances.

'That's the room, you know,' he said, nodding in the direction of the open door, and dropping his voice to a whisper.

'Yes, I know,' I replied.

'What you've been trying to shut it already, have you? Well, you are a game one!' And with this complementary if not very respectful comment he hastened out of the house. Evidently he had no intention of proffering his services towards the solution of the mystery.

I cast one glance at the door—it stood wide open. Through the windows I had left bare to the night, moonlight was beginning to stream cold and silvery. Before I did aught else I felt I must write to Mr Carrison and Patty, so straightway I hurried to one of the great tables in the hall, and lighting a candle my thoughtful link girl had provided, with many other things, sat down and dashed off the two epistles.

Then down the long avenue, with its mysterious lights and shades, with the moonbeams glinting here and there, playing at hide-and-seek round the boles of the trees and through the tracery of quivering leaf and stem, I walked as fast as if I were doing a match against time.

It was delicious, the scent of the summer odours, the smell of the earth; if it had not been for the door I should have felt too happy. As it was—'Look here, Phil,' I said, all of a sudden; 'life's not child's play, as uncle truly remarks. That door is just the trouble you have now to face, and you must face it! But for that door you would never have been here. I hope you are not going to turn coward the very first night. Courage!—that is your enemy—conquer it.'

'I will try,' my other self answered back. 'I can but try. I can but fail.'

The post-office was at Ladlow Hollow, a little hamlet through which the stream I had remarked dawdling on its way across the park flowed swiftly, spanned by an ancient bridge.

As I stood by the door of the little shop, asking some questions of the postmistress, the same gentleman I had met in the afternoon mounted on his roan horse, passed on foot. He wished me goodnight as he went by, and nodded familiarly to my companion, who curtseyed her acknowledgements.

'His lordship ages fast,' she remarked, following the retreating figure with her eyes.

'His lordship,' I repeated. 'Of whom are you speaking?'

'Of Lord Ladlow,' she said.

'Oh! I have never seen him,' I answered, puzzled.

'Why, that was Lord Ladlow!' she exclaimed.

You may be sure I had something to think about as I walked back to the Hall—something beside the moonlight and the sweet night-scents, and the rustle of beast and bird and leaf, that make silence seem more eloquent than noise away down in the heart of the country.

26

Lord Ladlow! my word, I thought he was hundreds, thousands of miles away; and here I find him—he walking in the opposite direction from his own home—I an inmate of his desolate abode. Hi!—what was that? I heard a noise in a shrubbery close at hand, and in an instant I was in the thick of the underwood. Something shot out and darted into the cover of the further plantation. I followed, but I could catch never a glimpse of it. I did not know the lie of the ground sufficiently to course with success, and I had at length to give up the hunt—heated, baffled, and annoyed.

When I got into the house the moon's beams were streaming down upon the hall; I could see every statue, every square of marble, every piece of armour. For all the world it seemed to me like something in a dream; but I was tired and sleepy, and decided I would not trouble about fire or food, or the open door, till the next morning: I would go to sleep.

With this intention I picked up some of my traps and carried them to a room on the first floor I had selected as small and habitable. I went down for the rest, and this time chanced to lay my hand on my rifle.

It was wet. I touched the floor—it was wet likewise.

I never felt anything like the thrill of delight which shot through me. I had to deal with flesh and blood, and I would deal with it, heaven helping me.

The next morning broke clear and bright. I was up with the lark— had washed, dressed, breakfasted, explored the house before the postman came with my letters.

One from Mr Carrison, one from Patty, and one from my uncle: I gave the man half a crown, I was so delighted, and said I was afraid my being at the Hall would cause him some additional trouble.

'No, sir,' he answered, profuse in his expressions of gratitude; 'I pass here every morning on my way to her ladyship's.'

'Who is her ladyship?' I asked.

'The Dowager Lady Ladlow,' he answered—'the old lord's widow.'

'And where is her place?' I persisted.

'If you keep on through the shrubbery and across the waterfall, you come to the house about a quarter of a mile further up the stream.'

He departed, after telling me there was only one post a day; and I hurried back to the room in which I had breakfasted, carrying my letters with me.

I opened Mr Carrison's first. The gist of it was, 'Spare no expense; if you run short of money telegraph for it.'

I opened my uncle's next. He implored me to return; he had always thought me hair-brained, but he felt a deep interest in and affection for me, and thought he could get me a good berth if I would only try to settle down and promise to stick to my work. The last was from Patty. O Patty, God bless you! Such women, I fancy, the men who fight best in battle, who stick last to a sinking ship, who are firm in life's struggles, who are brave to resist temptation, must have known and loved. I can't tell you more about the letter, except that it gave me strength to go on to the end.

I spent the forenoon considering that door. I looked at it from within and from without. I eyed it critically. I tried whether there was any reason why it should fly open, and I found that so long as I remained on the threshold it remained closed; if I walked even so far away as the opposite side of the hall, it swung wide.

Do what I would, it burst from latch and bolt. I could not lock it because there was no key.

28

Well, before two o'clock I confess I was baffled.

At two there came a visitor—none other than Lord Ladlow himself. Sorely I wanted to take his horse round to the stables, but he would not hear of it.

'Walk beside me across the park, if you will be so kind,' he said; 'I want to speak to you.

We went together across the park, and before we parted I felt I could have gone through fire and water for this simple-spoken nobleman.

'You must not stay here ignorant of the rumours which are afloat,' he said. 'Of course, when I let the place to Mr Carrison I knew nothing of the open door.'

'Did you not, sir?—my lord, I mean,' I stammered.

He smiled. 'Do not trouble yourself about my title, which, indeed, carries a very empty state with it, but talk to me as you might to a friend. I had no idea there was any ghost story connected with the Hall, or I should have kept the place empty.'

I did not exactly know what to answer, so I remained silent.

'How did you chance to be sent here?' he asked, after a pause.

I told him. When the first shock was over, a lord did not seem very different from anybody else. If an emperor had taken a morning canter across the park, I might, supposing him equally affable, have spoken as familiarly to him as to Lord Ladlow. My mother always said I entirely lacked the bump of veneration! Beginning at the beginning, I repeated the whole story, from Parton's remark about the sovereign to Mr Carrison's conversation with my uncle. When I had left London behind in the narrative, however, and arrived at

29

the Hall, I became somewhat more reticent. After all, it was his Hall people could not live in—his door that would not keep shut; and it seemed to me these were facts he might dislike being forced upon his attention.

But he would have it. What had I seen? What did I think of the matter? Very honestly I told him I did not know what to say. The door certainly would not remain shut, and there seemed no human agency to account for its persistent opening; but then, on the other hand, ghosts generally did not tamper with firearms, and my rifle, though not loaded, had been tampered with—I was sure of that.

My companion listened attentively. 'You are not frightened, are you?' he enquired at length.

'Not now,' I answered. 'The door did give me a start last evening, but I am not afraid of that since I find someone else is afraid of a bullet.'

He did not answer for a minute; then he said:

'The theory people have set up about the open door is this: As in that room my uncle was murdered, they say the door will never remain shut till the murderer is discovered.'

'Murdered!' I did not like the word at all; it made me feel chill and uncomfortable.

'Yes—he was murdered sitting in his chair, and the assassin has never been discovered. At first mans persons inclined to the belief that I killed him; indeed, many are of that opinion still.'

'But you did not, sir—there is not a word of truth in that story, is there?'

He laid his hand on my shoulder as he said:

'No, my lad; not a word. I loved the old man tenderly. Even when he disinherited me for the sake of his young wife, I was sorry, but not angry; and when he sent for me and assured me he had resolved to repair that wrong, I tried to induce him to leave the lady a handsome sum in addition to her jointure. "If you do not, people may think she has not been the source of happiness you expected," I added.

"Thank you, Hal," he said. "You are a good fellow; we will talk further about this tomorrow."

And then he bade me goodnight.

'Before morning broke—it was in the summer two years ago—the household was aroused by a fearful scream. It was his death-cry. He had been stabbed from behind in the neck. He was seated in his chair writing—writing a letter to me. But for that I might have found it harder to clear myself than was in the case; for his solicitors came forward and said he had signed a will leaving all his personalty to me—he was very rich—unconditionally, only three days previously. That, of course, supplied the motive, as my lady's lawyer put it. She was very vindictive, spared no expense in trying to prove my guilt, and said openly she would never rest till she saw justice done, if it cost her the whole of her fortune. The letter lying before the dead man, over which blood had spurted, she declared must have been placed on his table by me; but the coroner saw there was an animus in this, for the few opening lines stated my uncle's desire to confide in me his reasons for changing his will— reasons, he said, that involved his honour, as they had destroyed his peace. "In the statement you will find sealed up with my will in—" At that point he was dealt his death-blow. The papers were never found, and the will was never proved. My lady put in the former will, leaving her everything. Ill as I could afford to go to law, I was obliged to dispute the matter, and the lawyers are at it still, and very likely will continue at it for years.

31

When I lost my good name, I lost my good health, and had to go abroad; and while I was away Mr Carrison took the Hall. Till I returned, I never heard a word about the open door. My solicitor said Mr Carrison was behaving badly; but I think now I must see them or him, and consider what can be done in the affair. As for yourself, it is of vital importance to me that this mystery should be cleared up, and if you are really not timid, stay on. I am too poor to make rash promises, but you won't find me ungrateful.'

'Oh, my lord!' I cried—the address slipped quite easily and naturally off my tongue—'I don't want any more money or anything, if I can only show Patty's father I am good for something—'

'Who is Patty?' he asked.

He read the answer in my face, for he said no more.

'Should you like to have a good dog for company?' he enquired after a pause.

I hesitated; then I said:

'No, thank you. I would rather watch and hunt for myself.'

And as I spoke, the remembrance of that 'something' in the shrubbery recurred to me, and I told him I thought there had been someone about the place the previous evening.

'Poachers,' he suggested; but I shook my head.

'A girl or a woman I imagine. However, I think a dog might hamper me.'

He went away, and I returned to the house. I never left it all day. I did not go into the garden, or the stable-yard, or the shrubbery, or anywhere; I devoted myself solely and exclusively to that door.

If I shut it once, I shut it a hundred times, and always with the same result. Do what I would, it swung wide. Never, however, when I was looking at it. So long as I could endure to remain, it stayed shut — the instant I turned my back, it stood open.

About four o'clock I had another visitor; no other than Lord Ladlow's daughter — the Honourable Beatrice, riding her funny little white pony.

She was a beautiful girl of fifteen or thereabouts, and she had the sweetest smile you ever saw.

'Papa sent me with this,' she said; 'he would not trust any other messenger,' and she put a piece of paper in my hand.

'Keep your food under lock and key; buy what you require yourself. Get your water from the pump in the stable-yard. I am going from home; but if you want anything, go or send to my daughter.'

'Any answer?' she asked, patting her pony's neck.

'Tell his lordship, if you please, I will "keep my powder dry"!' I replied.

'You have made papa look so happy,' she said, still patting that fortunate pony.

'If it is in my power, I will make him look happier still, Miss —-' and I hesitated, not knowing how to address her.

'Call me Beatrice,' she said, with an enchanting grace; then added, slily, 'Papa promises me I shall be introduced to Patty ere long,' and before I could recover from my astonishment, she had tightened the bit and was turning across the park.

'One moment, please,' I cried. 'You can do something for me.'

'What is it?' and she came back, trotting over the great sweep in front of the house.

'Lend me your pony for a minute.'

She was off before I could even offer to help her alight—off, and gathering up her habit dexterously with one hand, led the docile old sheep forward with the other.

I took the bridle—when I was with horses I felt amongst my own kind— stroked the pony, pulled his ears, and let him thrust his nose into my hand.

Miss Beatrice is a countess now, and a happy wife and mother; but I sometimes see her, and the other night she took me carefully into a conservatory and asked:

'Do you remember Toddy, Mr Edlyd?'

'Remember him!' I exclaimed; 'I can never forget him!'

'He is dead!' she told me, and there were tears in her beautiful eyes as she spoke the words.

'Mr Edlyd, I loved Toddy!'

Well, I took Toddy up to the house, and under the third window to the right hand. He was a docile creature, and let me stand on the saddle while I looked into the only room in Ladlow Hall I had been unable to enter.

It was perfectly bare of furniture, there was not a thing in it—not a chair or table, not a picture on the walls, or ornament on the chimney-piece.

'That is where my grand-uncle's valet slept,' said Miss Beatrice. 'It was he who first ran in to help him the night he was murdered.'

'Where is the valet?' I asked.

'Dead,' she answered. 'The shock killed him. He loved his master more than he loved himself.'

I had seen all I wished, so I jumped off the saddle, which I had carefully dusted with a branch plucked from a lilac tree; between jest and earnest pressed the hem of Miss Beatrice's habit to my lips as I arranged its folds; saw her wave her hand as she went at a hand-gallop across the park; and then turned back once again into the lonely house, with the determination to solve the mystery attached to it or die in the attempt.

Why, I cannot explain, but before I went to bed that night I drove a gimlet I found in the stables hard into the floor, and said to the door:

'Now I am keeping you open.'

When I went down in the morning the door was close shut, and the handle of the gimlet, broken off short, lying in the hall.

I put my hand to wipe my forehead; it was dripping with perspiration. I did not know what to make of the place at all! I went out into the open air for a few minutes; when I returned the door again stood wide.

If I were to pursue in detail the days and nights that followed, I should weary my readers. I can only say they changed my life. The solitude, the solemnity, the mystery, produced an effect I do not profess to understand, but that I cannot regret.

I have hesitated about writing of the end, but it must come, so let me hasten to it.

Though feeling convinced that no human agency did or could keep the door open, I was certain that some living person had means of access to the house which I could not discover, This was made apparent in trifles which might well have escaped unnoticed had several, or even two people occupied the mansion, but that in my solitary position it was impossible to overlook. A chair would be misplaced, for instance; a path would be visible over a dusty floor; my papers I found were moved; my clothes touched—letters I carried about with me, and kept under my pillow at night; still, the fact remained that when I went to the post-office, and while I was asleep, someone did wander over the house. On Lord Ladlow's return I meant to ask him for some further particulars of his uncle's death, and I was about to write to Mr Carrison and beg permission to have the door where the valet had slept broken open, when one morning, very early indeed, I spied a hairpin lying close beside it.

What an idiot I had been! If I wanted to solve the mystery of the open door, of course I must keep watch in the room itself. The door would not stay wide unless there was a reason for it, and most certainly a hairpin could not have got into the house without assistance.

I made up my mind what I should do—that I would go to the post early, and take up my position about the hour I had hitherto started for Ladlow Hollow. I felt on the eve of a discovery, and longed for the day to pass, that the night might come.

It was a lovely morning; the weather had been exquisite during the whole week, and I flung the hall-door wide to let in the sunshine

36

and the breeze. As I did so, I saw there was a basket on the top step—a basket filled with rare and beautiful fruit and flowers.

Mr Carrison had let off the gardens attached to Ladlow Hall for the season—he thought he might as well save something out of the fire, he said, so my fare had not been varied with delicacies of that kind. I was very fond of fruit in those days, and seeing a card addressed to me, I instantly selected a tempting peach, and ate it a little greedily perhaps.

I might say I had barely swallowed the last morsel, when Lord Ladlow's caution recurred to me. The fruit had a curious flavour— there was a strange taste hanging about my palate. For a moment, sky, trees and park swam before my eyes; then I made up my mind what to do.

I smelt the fruit—it had all the same faint odour; then I put some in my pocket—took the basket and locked it away—walked round to the farmyard—asked for the loan of a horse that was generally driven in a light cart, and in less than half an hour was asking in Ladlow to be directed to a doctor.

Rather cross at being disturbed so early, he was at first inclined to pooh-pooh my idea; but I made him cut open a pear and satisfy himself the fruit had been tampered with.

'It is fortunate you stopped at the first peach,' he remarked, after giving me a draught, and some medicine to take back, and advising me to keep in the open air as much as possible. 'I should like to retain this fruit and see you again tomorrow.'

We did not think then on how many morrows we should see each other!

Riding across to Ladlow, the postman had given me three letters, but I did not read them till I was seated under a great tree in the park, with a basin of milk and a piece of bread beside me.

Hitherto, there had been nothing exciting in my correspondence. Patty's epistles were always delightful, but they could not be regarded as sensational; and about Mr Carrison's there was a monotony I had begun to find tedious. On this occasion, however, no fault could be found on that score. The contents of his letter greatly surprised me. He said Lord Ladlow had released him from his bargain—that I could, therefore, leave the Hall at once. He enclosed me ten pounds, and said he would consider how he could best advance my interests; and that I had better call upon him at his private house when I returned to London.

'I do not think I shall leave Ladlow yet awhile,' I considered, as I replaced his letter in its envelope. 'Before I go I should like to make it hot for whoever sent me that fruit; so unless Lord Ladlow turns me out I'll stay a little longer.'

Lord Ladlow did not wish me to leave. The third letter was from him.

'I shall return home tomorrow night,' he wrote, 'and see you on Wednesday. I have arranged satisfactorily with Mr Carrison, and as the Hall is my own again, I mean to try to solve the mystery it contains myself. If you choose to stop and help me to do so, you would confer a favour, and I will try to make it worth your while.'

'I will keep watch tonight, and see if I cannot give you some news tomorrow,' I thought. And then I opened Patty's letter—the best, dearest, sweetest letter any postman in all the world could have brought me.

If it had not been for what Lord Ladlow said about his sharing my undertaking, I should not have chosen that night for my vigil. I felt ill and languid—fancy, no doubt, to a great degree inducing these

38

sensations. I had lost energy in a most unaccountable manner. The long, lonely days had told upon my spirits—the fidgety feeling which took me a hundred times in the twelve hours to look upon the open door, to close it, and to count how many steps I could take before it opened again, had tried my mental strength as a perpetual blister might have worn away my physical. In no sense was I fit for the task I had set myself, and yet I determined to go through with it. Why had I never before decided to watch in that mysterious chamber? Had I been at the bottom of my heart afraid? In the bravest of us there are depths of cowardice that lurk unsuspected till they engulf our courage.

The day wore on—the long, dreary day; evening approached—the night shadows closed over the Hall. The moon would not rise for a couple of hours more. Everything was still as death. The house had never before seemed to me so silent and so deserted.

I took a light, and went up to my accustomed room, moving about for a time as though preparing for bed; then I extinguished the candle, softly opened the door, turned the key, and put it in my pocket, slipped softly downstairs, across the hail, through the open door. Then I knew I had been afraid, for I felt a thrill of terror as in the dark I stepped over the threshold. I paused and listened—there was not a sound—the night was still and sultry, as though a storm were brewing.

Not a leaf seemed moving—the very mice remained in their holes! Noiselessly I made my way to the other side of the room. There was an old-fashioned easy-chair between the bookshelves and the bed; I sat down in it, shrouded by the heavy curtain.

The hours passed—were ever hours so long? The moon rose, came and looked in at the windows, and then sailed away to the west; but not a sound, no, not even the cry of a bird. I seemed to myself a mere collection of nerves. Every part of my body appeared twitching. It was agony to remain still; the desire to move became a form of torture. Ah! a streak in the sky; morning at last, Heaven be praised! Had ever anyone before so welcomed the dawn? A thrush began to sing—was there ever heard such delightful music? It was the morning twilight, soon the sun would rise; soon that awful vigil would be over, and yet I was no nearer the mystery than before. Hush! what was that? It had come. After the hours of watching and waiting; after the long night and the long suspense, it came in a moment.

The locked door opened—so suddenly, so silently, that I had barely time to draw back behind the curtain, before I saw a woman in the room. She went straight across to the other door and closed it, securing it as I saw with bolt and lock. Then just glancing around, she made her way to the cabinet, and with a key she produced shot back the wards. I did not stir, I scarcely breathed, and yet she seemed uneasy. Whatever she wanted to do she evidently was in haste to finish, for she took out the drawers one by one, and placed them on the floor; then, as the light grew better, I saw her first kneel on the floor, and peer into every aperture, and subsequently repeat the same process, standing on a chair she drew forward for the purpose. A slight, lithe woman, not a lady, clad all in black—not a bit of white about her. What on earth could she want? In a moment it flashed upon me—THE WILL AND THE LETTER! SHE IS SEARCHING FOR THEM.

I sprang from my concealment—I had her in my grasp; but she tore herself out of my hands, fighting like a wild-cat: she hit, scratched, kicked, shifting her body as though she had not a bone in it, and at last slipped herself free, and ran wildly towards the door by which she had entered.

If she reached it, she would escape me. I rushed across the room and just caught her dress as she was on the threshold. My blood was up, and I dragged her back: she had the strength of twenty devils, I think, and struggled as surely no woman ever did before.

'I do not want to kill you,' I managed to say in gasps, 'but I will if you do not keep quiet.'

'Bah!' she cried; and before I knew what she was doing she had the revolver out of my pocket and fired.

She missed: the ball just glanced off my sleeve. I fell upon her—I can use no other expression, for it had become a fight for life, and no man can tell the ferocity there is in him till he is placed as I was then—fell upon her, and seized the weapon. She would not let it go, but I held her so tight she could not use it. She bit my face; with her disengaged hand she tore my hair. She turned and twisted and slipped about like a snake, but I did not feel pain or anything except a deadly horror lest my strength should give out.

Could I hold out much longer? She made one desperate plunge, I felt the grasp with which I held her slackening; she felt it too, and seizing her advantage tore herself free, and at the same instant fired again blindly, and again missed.

Suddenly there came a look of horror into her eyes—a frozen expression of fear.

'See!' she cried; and flinging the revolver at me, fled.

I saw, as in a momentary flash, that the door I had beheld locked stood wide—that there stood beside the table an awful figure, with uplifted hand—and then I saw no more. I was struck at last; as she threw the revolver at me she must have pulled the trigger, for I felt something like red-hot iron enter my shoulder, and I could but rush from the room before I fell senseless on the marble pavement of the ball.

When the postman came that morning, finding no one stirring, be looked through one of the long windows that flanked the door; then he ran to the farmyard and called for help.

'There is something wrong inside,' be cried. 'That young gentleman is lying on the floor in a pool of blood.'

As they rushed round to the front of the house they saw Lord Ladlow riding up the avenue, and breathlessly told him what had happened.

'Smash in one of the windows,' be said; 'and go instantly for a doctor.'

They laid me on the bed in that terrible room, and telegraphed for my father. For long I hovered between life and death, but at length I recovered sufficiently to be removed to the house Lord Ladlow owned on the other side of the Hollow.

Before that time I had told him all I knew, and begged him to make instant search for the will.

'Break up the cabinet if necessary,' I entreated, 'I am sure the papers are there.'

And they were. His lordship got his own, and as to the scandal and the crime, one was hushed up and the other remained unpunished. The dowager and her maid went abroad the very morning I lay on the marble pavement at Ladlow Hall—they never returned.

My lord made that one condition of his silence.

Not in Meadowshire, but in a fairer county still, I have a farm which I manage, and make both ends meet comfortably.

Patty is the best wife any man ever possessed—and I—well, I am just as happy if a trifle more serious than of old; but there are times when a great horror of darkness seems to fall upon me, and at such periods I cannot endure to be left alone.

THE OLD HOUSE IN VAUXHALL WALK

CHAPTER ONE

'Houseless—homeless—hopeless!'

Many a one who had before him trodden that same street must have uttered the same words—-the weary, the desolate, the hungry, the forsaken, the waifs and strays of struggling humanity that are always coming and going, cold, starving and miserable, over the pavements of Lambeth Parish; but it is open to question whether they were ever previously spoken with a more thorough conviction of their truth, or with a feeling of keener self-pity, than by the young man who hurried along Vauxhall Walk one rainy winter's night, with no overcoat on his shoulders and no hat on his head.

A strange sentence for one-and-twenty to give expression to—and it was stranger still to come from the lips of a person who looked like and who was a gentleman. He did not appear either to have sunk very far down in the good graces of Fortune. There was no sign or token which would have induced a passer-by to imagine he had been worsted after a long fight with calamity. His boots were not worn down at the heels or broken at the toes, as many, many boots were which dragged and shuffled and scraped along the pavement. His clothes were good and fashionably cut, and innocent of the rents and patches and tatters that slunk wretchedly by, crouched in doorways, and held out a hand mutely appealing for charity. His face was not pinched with famine or lined with wicked wrinkles, or brutalised by drink and debauchery, and yet he said and thought he was hopeless, and almost in his young despair spoke the words aloud.

43

It was a bad night to be about with such a feeling in one's heart. The rain was cold, pitiless and increasing. A damp, keen wind blew down the cross streets leading from the river. The fumes of the gas works seemed to fall with the rain. The roadway was muddy; the pavement greasy; the lamps burned dimly; and that dreary district of London looked its very gloomiest and worst.

Certainly not an evening to be abroad without a home to go to, or a sixpence in one's pocket, yet this was the position of the young gentleman who, without a hat, strode along Vauxhall Walk, the rain beating on his unprotected head.

Upon the houses, so large and good—once inhabited by well-to-do citizens, now let out for the most part in floors to weekly tenants—he looked enviously. He would have given much to have had a room, or even part of one. He had been walking for a long time, ever since dark in fact, bind dark falls soon in December. He was tired and cold and hungry, and he saw no prospect save of pacing the streets all night.

As he passed one of the lamps, the light falling on his face revealed handsome young features, a mobile, sensitive mouth, and that particular formation of the eyebrows—not a frown exactly, but a certain draw of the brows—often considered to bespeak genius, but which more surely accompanies an impulsive organisation easily pleased, easily depressed, capable of suffering very keenly or of enjoying fully. In his short life he had not enjoyed much, and he had suffered a good deal. That night, when he walked bareheaded through the rain, affairs had come to a crisis.

So far as he in his despair felt able to see or reason, the best thing he could do was to die. The world did not want him; he would be better out of it.

The door of one of the houses stood open, and he could see in the dimly lighted hall some few articles of furniture waiting to be removed. A van stood beside the curb, and two men were lifting a table into it as he, for a second, paused.

'Ah,' he thought, 'even those poor people have some place to go to, some shelter provided, while I have not a roof to cover my head, or a shilling to get a night's lodging.' And he went on fast, as if memory were spurring him, so fast that a man running after had some trouble to overtake him.

'Master Graham! Master Graham!' this man exclaimed, breathlessly; arid, thus addressed, the young fellow stopped as if he had been shot.

'Who are you that know me?' he asked, facing round.

'I'm William; don't you remember William, Master Graham? And, Lord's sake, sir, what are you doing out a night like this without your hat?'

'I forgot it,' was the answer; 'and I did not care to go back and fetch it.'

'Then why don't you buy another, sir? You'll catch your death of cold; and besides, you'll excuse me, sir, but it does look odd.'

'I know that,' said Master Graham grimly; 'but I haven't a halfpenny in the world.'

'Have you and the master, then—' began the man, but there he hesitated and stopped.

'Had a quarrel? Yes, and one that will last us our lives,' finished the other, with a bitter laugh.

'And where are you going now?'

'Going! Nowhere, except to seek out the softest paving stone, or the shelter of an arch.'

'You are joking, sir.'

'I don't feel much in a mood for jesting either.'

'Will you come back with me, Master Graham? We are just at the last of our moving, but there is a spark of fire still in the grate, and it would be better talking out of this rain. Will you come, sir?'

'Come! Of course I will come,' said the young fellow, and, turning, they retraced their steps to the house he had looked into as he passed along.

An old, old house, with long, wide hall, stairs low, easy of ascent, with deep cornices to the ceilings, and oak floorings, and mahogany doors, which still spoke mutely of the wealth and stability of the original owner, who lived before the Tradescants and Ashmoles were thought of, arid had been sleeping far hnger than they, in St Mary's churchyard, hard by the archbishop's palace.

'Step upstairs, sir,' entreated the departing tenant; 'it's cold down here, with the door standing wide.'

'Had you the whole house, then, William?' asked Graham Coulton, in some surprise.

'The whole of it, and right sorry I, for one, am to leave it; but nothing else would serve my wife. This room, sir,' and with a little conscious pride, William, doing the honours of his late residence, asked his guest into a spacious apartment occupying the full width of the house on the first floor.

Tired though he was, the young man could not repress an exclamation of astonishment.

'Why, we have nothing so large as this at home, William,' he said.

'It's a fine house,' answered William, raking the embers together as he spoke and throwing some wood upon them; 'but, like many a good family, it has come down in the world.'

There were four windows in the room, shuttered close; they had deep, low seats, suggestive of pleasant days gone by; when, well-curtained and well-cushioned, they formed snug retreats for the children, and sometimes for adults also; there was no furniture left, unless an oaken settle beside the hearth, and a large mirror let into the panelling at the opposite end of the apartment, with a black marble console table beneath it, could be so considered; but the very absence of chairs and tables enabled the magnificent proportions of the chamber to be seen to full advantage, and there was nothing to distract the attention from the ornamented ceiling, the panelled walls, the old-world chimney-piece so quaintly carved, and the fireplace lined with tiles, each one of which contained a picture of some scriptural or allegorical subject.

'Had you been staying on here, William,' said Coulton, flinging himself wearily on the settle, 'I'd have asked you to let me stop where I am for the night.'

'If you can make shift, sir, there is nothing as I am aware of to prevent you stopping,' answered the man, fanning the wood into a flame. 'I shan't take the key back to the landlord till tomorrow, and this would be better for you than the cold streets at any rate.'

'Do you really mean what you say?' asked the other eagerly. 'I should be thankful to lie here; I feel dead beat.'

'Then stay, Master Graham, and welcome. I'll fetch a basket of coals I was going to put in the van, and make up a good fire, so that you can warm yourself then I must run round to the other house for a minute or two, but it's not far, and I'll be back as soon as ever I can.'

'Thank you, William; you were always good to me,' said the young man gratefully. 'This is delightful,' and he stretched his numbed hands over the blazing wood, and looked round the room with a satisfied smile.

'I did not expect to get into such quarters,' he remarked, as his friend in need reappeared, carrying a half-bushel basket full of coals, with which he proceeded to make up a roaring fire. 'I am sure the last thing I could have imagined was meeting with anyone I knew in Vauxhall Walk.'

'Where were you coming from, Master Graham?' asked William curiously.

'From old Melfield's. I was at his school once, you know, and he has now retired, and is living upon the proceeds of years of robbery in Kennington Oval. I thought, perhaps he would lend me a pound, or offer me a night's lodging, or even a glass of wine; but, oh dear, no. He took the moral tone, and observed he could have nothing to say to a son who defied his father's authority.

He gave me plenty of advice, but nothing else, and showed me out into the rain with a bland courtesy, for which I could have struck him.'

William muttered something under his breath which was not a blessing, and added aloud:

'You are better here, sir, I think, at any rate. I'll be back in less than half an hour.'

Left to himself, young Coulton took off his coat, and shifting the settle a little, hung it over the end to dry. With his handkerchief he rubbed some of the wet out of his hair; then, perfectly exhausted, he lay down before the fire and, pillowing his head on his arm, fell fast asleep.

He was awakened nearly an hour afterwards by the sound of someone gently stirring the fire and moving quietly about the room. Starting into a sitting posture, he looked around him, bewildered for a moment, and then, recognising his humble friend, said laughingly:

'I had lost myself; I could not imagine where I was.'

'I am sorry to see you here, sir,' was the reply; 'but still this is better than being out of doors. It has come on a nasty night. I brought a rug round with me that, perhaps, you would wrap yourself in.'

'I wish, at the same time, you had brought me something to eat,' said the young man, laughing.

'Are you hungry, then, sir?' asked William, in a tone of concern.

'Yes; I have had nothing to eat since breakfast. The governor and I commenced rowing the minute we sat down to luncheon, and I rose and left the table. But hunger does not signify; I am dry and warm, and can forget the other matter in sleep.'

'And it's too late now to buy anything,' soliloquised the man; 'the shops are all shut long ago.

Do you think, sir,' he added, brightening, 'you could manage some bread and cheese?'

'Do I think—I should call it a perfect feast,' answered Graham Coulton. 'But never mind about food tonight, William; you have had trouble enough, and to spare, already.'

William's only answer was to dart to the door and run downstairs. Presently he reappeared, carrying in one hand bread and cheese wrapped up in paper, and in the other a pewter measure full of beer.

49

'It's the best I could do, sir,' he said apologetically. 'I had to beg this from the landlady.'

'Here's to her good health!' exclaimed the young fellow gaily, taking a long pull at the tankard. 'That tastes better than champagne in my father's house.'

'Won't he be uneasy about you?' ventured William, who, having by this time emptied the coals, was now seated on the inverted basket, looking wistfully at the relish with which the son of the former master was eating his bread and cheese.

'No,' was the decided answer. 'When he hears it pouring cats and dogs he will only hope I am out in the deluge, and say a good drenching will cool my pride.'

'I do not think you are right there,' remarked the man.

'But I am sure I am. My father always hated me, as he hated my mother.'

'Begging your pardon, sir; he was over fond of your mother.'

'If you had heard what he said about her today, you might find reason to alter your opinion. He told me I resembled her in mind as well as body; that I was a coward, a simpleton, and a hypocrite.'

'He did not mean it, sir.'

'He did, every word. He does think I am a coward, because I—I—' And the young fellow broke into a passion of hysterical tears.

'I don't half like leaving you here alone,' said William, glancing round the room with a quick trouble in his eyes; 'but I have no place fit to ask you to stop, and I am forced to go myself, because I am night watchman, and must be on at twelve o'clock.'

'I shall be right enough,' was the answer. 'Only I mustn't talk any more of my father. Tell me about yourself, William. How did you manage to get such a big house, and why are you leaving it?'

'The landlord put me in charge, sir; and it was my wife's fancy not to like it.'

'Why did she not like it?'

'She felt desolate alone with the children at night,' answered William, turning away his head; then added, next minute: 'Now, sir, if you think I can do no more for you, I had best be off.

Time's getting on. I'll look round tomorrow morning.'

'Good night,' said the young fellow, stretching out his hand, which the other took as freely and frankly as it was offered. 'What should I have done this evening if I had not chanced to meet you?'

'I don't think there is much chance in the world, Master Graham,' was the quiet answer. 'I do hope you will rest well, and not be the worse for your wetting.'

'No fear of that,' was the rejoinder, and the next minute the young man found himself all alone in the Old House in Vauxhall Walk.

CHAPTER TWO

Lying on the settle, with the fire burnt out, and the room in total darkness, Graham Coulton dreamed a curious dream. He thought he awoke from deep slumber to find a log smouldering away upon the hearth, and the mirror at the end of the apartment reflecting fitful gleams of light.

He could not understand how it came to pass that, far away as he was from the glass, he was able to see everything in it; but he resigned himself to the difficulty without astonishment, as people generally do in dreams.

Neither did he feel surprised when he beheld the outline of a female figure seated beside the fire, engaged in picking something out of her lap and dropping it with a despairing gesture.

He heard the mellow sound of gold, and knew she was lifting and dropping sovereigns, lie turned a little so as to see the person engaged in such a singular and meaningless manner, and found that, where there had been no chair on the previous night, there was a chair now, on which was seated an old, wrinkled hag, her clothes poor and ragged, a mob cap barely covering her scant white hair, her cheeks sunken, her nose hooked, her fingers more like talons than aught else as they dived down into the heap of gold, portions of which they lifted but to scatter mournfully.

'Oh! my lost life,' she moaned, in a voice of the bitterest anguish. 'Oh! my lost life—for one day, for one hour of it again!'

Out of the darkness—out of the corner of the room where the shadows lay deepest—out from the gloom abiding near the door— out from the dreary night, with their sodden feet and wet dripping from their heads, came the old men and the young children, the worn women and the weary hearts, whose misery that gold might have relieved, but whose wretchedness it mocked.

Round that miser, who once sat gloating as she now sat lamenting, they crowded—all those pale, sad shapes—the aged of days, the infant of hours, the sobbing outcast, honest poverty, repentant vice;

52

but one low cry proceeded from those pale lips—a cry for help she might have given, but which she withheld.

They closed about her, all together, as they had done singly in life; they prayed, they sobbed, they entreated; with haggard eyes the figure regarded the poor she had repulsed, the children against whose cry she had closed her ears, the old people she had suffered to starve and die for want of what would have been the merest trifle to her; then, with a terrible scream, she raised her lean arms above her head, and sank down—down—the gold scattering as it fell out of her lap, and rolling along the floor, till its gleam was lost in the outer darkness beyond.

Then Graham Coulton awoke in good earnest, with the perspiration oozing from every pore, with a fear and an agony upon him such as he had never before felt in all his existence, and with the sound of the heart-rending cry—'Oh! my lost life'—still ringing in his ears.

Mingled with all, too, there seemed to have been some lesson for him which he had forgotten, that, try as he would, eluded his memory, and which, in the very act of waking, glided away.

He lay for a little thinking about all this, and then, still heavy with sleep, retraced his way into dreamland once more.

It was natural, perhaps, that, mingling with the strange fantasies which follow in the train of night and darkness, the former vision should recur, and the young man ere long found himself toiling through scene after scene wherein the figure of the woman he had seen seated beside a dying fire held principal place.

He saw her walking slowly across the floor munching a dry crust— she who could have purchased all the luxuries wealth can command; on the hearth, contemplating her, stood a man of commanding presence, dressed in the fashion of long ago. In his eyes there was a dark look of anger, on his lips a curling smile of disgust, and somehow, even in his sleep, the dreamer understood it was the ancestor to the descendant he beheld—that the house put to mean uses in which he lay had never so far descended from its high estate, as the woman possessed of so pitiful a soul, contaminated with the most despicable and insidious vice poor humanity knows, for all other vices seem to have connection with the flesh, but the greed of the miser eats into the very soul.

Filthy of person, repulsive to look at, hard of heart as she was, he yet beheld another phantom, which, coming into the room, met her almost on the threshold, taking her by the hand, and pleading, as it seemed, for assistance. He could not hear all that passed, but a word now and then fell upon his ear. Some talk of former days; some mention of a fair young mother—an appeal, as it seemed, to a time when they were tiny brother and sister, and the accursed greed for gold had not divided them. All in vain; the hag only answered him as she had answered the children, and the young girls, and the old people in his former vision. Her heart was as invulnerable to natural affection as it had proved to human sympathy. He begged, as it appeared, for aid to avert some bitter misfortune or terrible disgrace, and adamant might have been found more yielding to his prayer. Then the figure standing on the hearth changed to an angel, which folded its wings mournfully over its face, and the man, with bowed head, slowly left the room.

Even as he did so the scene changed again; it was night once more, and the miser wended her way upstairs. From below, Graham Coulton fancied he watched her toiling wearily from step to step. She had aged strangely since the previous scenes. She moved with difficulty; it seemed the greatest exertion for her to creep from step to step, her skinny hand traversing the balusters with slow and painful deliberateness. Fascinated, the young man's eyes followed the progress of that feeble, decrepit woman. She was solitary in a desolate house, with a deeper blackness than the darkness of night waiting to engulf her.

54

It seemed to Graham Coulton that after that he lay for a time in a still, dreamless sleep, upon awaking from which he found himself entering a chamber as sordid and unclean in its appointments as the woman of his previous vision had been in her person. The poorest labourer's wife would have gathered more comforts around her than that room contained. A four-poster bedstead without hangings of any kind—a blind drawn up awry—an old carpet covered with dust, and dirt on the floor—a rickety washstand with all the paint worn off it—an ancient mahogany dressing-table, and a cracked glass spotted all over—were all the objects he could at first discern, looking at the room through that dim light which oftentimes obtains in dreams.

By degrees, however, he perceived the outline of someone lying huddled on the bed. Drawing nearer, he found it was that of the person whose dreadful presence seemed to pervade the house.

What a terrible sight she looked, with her thin white locks scattered over the pillow, with what were mere remnants of blankets gathered about her shoulders, with her claw-like fingers clutching the clothes, as though even in sleep she was guarding her gold!

An awful and a repulsive spectacle, but not with half the terror in it of that which followed.

Even as the young man looked he heard stealthy footsteps on the stairs. Then he saw first one man and then his fellow steal cautiously into the room. Another second, and the pair stood beside the bed, murder in their eyes.

Graham Coulton tried to shout—tried to move, but the deterrent power which exists in dreams only tied his tongue and paralysed his limbs. He could but hear and look, and what he heard and saw was this: aroused suddenly from sleep, the woman started, only to receive a blow from one of the ruffians, whose fellow followed his lead by plunging a knife into her breast.

Then, with a gurgling scream, she fell back on the bed, and at the same moment, with a cry, Graham Coulton again awoke, to thank heaven it was but an illusion.

CHAPTER THREE

'I hope you slept well, sir.' It was William, who, coming into the hall with the sunlight of a fine bright morning streaming after him, asked this question: 'Had you a good night's rest?'

Graham Coulton laughed, and answered:

'Why, faith, I was somewhat in the case of Paddy, "who could not slape for dhraming". I slept well enough, I suppose, but whether it was in consequence of the row with my dad, or the hard bed, or the cheese— most likely the bread and cheese so late at night—I dreamt all the night long, the most extraordinary dreams. Some old woman kept cropping up, and I saw her murdered.'

'You don't say that, sir?' said William nervously.

'I do, indeed,' was the reply. 'However, that is all gone and past. I have been down in the kitchen and had a good wash, and I am as fresh as a daisy, and as hungry as a hunter; and, oh, William, can you get mc any breakfast?'

'Certainly, Master Graham. I have brought round a kettle, and I will make the water boil immediately. I suppose, sir'—this tentatively— 'you'll be going home today?'

'Home!' repeated the young man. 'Decidedly not. I'll never go home again till I return with some medal hung to my coat, or a leg or arm

56

cut off. I've thought it all out, William. I'll go and enlist. There's a talk of war; and, living or dead, my father shall have reason to retract his opinion about my being a coward.'

'I am sure the admiral never thought you anything of the sort, sir,' said William. 'Why, you have the pluck of ten!'

'Not before him,' answered the young fellow sadly.

'You'll do nothing rash, Master Graham; you won't go 'listing, or aught of that sort, in your anger?'

'If I do not, what is to become of me?' asked the other. 'I cannot dig—to beg I am ashamed.

Why, but for you, I should not have had a roof over my head last night.'

'Not much of a roof, I am afraid, sir.'

'Not much of a roof!' repeated the young man. 'Why, who could desire a better? What a capital room this is,' he went on, looking around the apartment, where William was now kindling a fire; 'one might dine twenty people here easily!'

'If you think so well of the place, Master Graham, you might stay here for a while, till you have made up your mind what you are going to do. The landlord won't make any objection, I am very sure.'

'Oh! nonsense; he would want a long rent for a house like this.'

'I dare say; if he could get it,' was William's significant answer.

'What do you mean? Won't the place let?'

'No, sir. I did not tell you last night, but there was a murder done here, and people are shy of the house ever since.'

'A murder! What sort of a murder? Who was murdered?'

'A woman, Master Graham—the landlord's sister; she lived here all alone, and was supposed to have money. Whether she had or hot, she was found dead from a stab in her breast, and if there ever was any money, it must have been taken at the same time, for none ever was found in the house from that day to this.'

'Was that the reason your wife would not stop here?' asked the young man, leaning against the mantelshelf, and looking thoughtfully down on William.

'Yes, sir. She could not stand it any longer; she got that thin and nervous one would have believed it possible; she never saw anything, but she said she heard footsteps and voices, and then when she walked through the hall, or up the staircase, someone always seemed to be following her. We put the children to sleep in that big room you had last night, and they declared they often saw an old woman sitting by the hearth. Nothing ever came my way, finished William, with a laugh; 'I was always ready to go to sleep the minute my head touched the pillow.'

'Were not the murderers discovered?' asked Graham Coulton.

'No, sir; the landlord, Miss Tynan's brother, had always lain under the suspicion of it—quite wrongfully, I am very sure—but he will never clear himself now. It was known he came and asked her for help a day or two before the murder, and it was also known he was able within a week or two to weather whatever trouble had been harassing him. Then, you see, the money was never found; and, altogether, people scarce knew what to think.'

'Humph!' ejaculated Graham Coulton, and he took a few turns up and down the apartment.

'Could I go and see this landlord?'

'Surely, sir, if you had a hat,' answered William, with such a serious decorum that the young man burst out laughing.

'That is an obstacle, certainly,' he remarked, 'and I must make a note do instead. I have a pencil in my pocket, so here goes.'

Within half an hour from the dispatch of that note William was back again with a sovereign; the landlord's compliments, and he would be much obliged if Mr Coulton could 'step round'.

'You'll do nothing rash, sir,' entreated William.

'Why, man,' answered the young fellow, 'one may as well be picked off by a ghost as a bullet.

What is there to be afraid of?'

William only shook his head. He did not think his young master was made of the stuff likely to remain alone in a haunted house and solve the mystery it assuredly contained by dint of his own unassisted endeavours. And yet when Graham Coulton came out of the landlord's house he looked more bright and gay than usual, and walked up the Lambeth road to the place where William awaited his return, humming an air as he paced along.

'We have settled the matter,' he said. 'And now if the dad wants his son for Christmas, it will trouble him to find him.'

'Don't say that, Master Graham, don't,' entreated the man, with a shiver; 'maybe after all it would have been better if you had never happened to chance upon Vauxhall Walk.'

'Don't croak, William,' answered the young man; 'if it was not the best day's work I ever did for myself I'm a Dutchman.'

During the whole of that forenoon and afternoon, Graham Coulton searched diligently for the missing treasurc Mr Tynan assured him had never been discovered. Youth is confident and self-opinionated, and this fresh explorer felt satisfied that, though others had failed, he would be successful. On the second floor he found one door locked, but he did not pay much attention to that at the moment, as he believed if there was anything concealed it was more likely to be found in the lower than the upper part of the house. Late into the evening he pursued his researches in the kitchen and cellars and old-fashioned cupboards, of which the basement had an abundance.

It was nearly eleven, when, engaged in poking about amongst the empty bins of a wine cellar as large as a family vault, he suddenly felt a rush of cold air at his back. Moving, his candle was instantly extinguished, and in the very moment of being left in darkness he saw, standing in the doorway, a woman, resembling her who had haunted his dreams overnight.

He rushed with outstretched hands to seize her, but clutched only air. He relit his candle, and closely examined the basement, shutting off communication with the ground floor ere doing so.

All in vain. Not a trace could he find of living creature—not a window was open—not a door unbolted.

'It is very odd,' he thought, as, after securely fastening the door at the top of the staircase, he searched the whole upper portion of the house, with the exception of the one room mentioned.

'I must get the key of that tomorrow,' he decided, standing gloomily with his back to the fire and his eyes wandering about the drawing-room, where he had once again taken up his abode.

Even as the thought passed through his mind, he saw standing in the open doorway a woman with white dishevelled hair, clad in mean garments, ragged and dirty. She lifted her hand and shook it at him with a menacing gesture, and then, just as he was darting towards her, a wonderful thing occurred.

From behind the great mirror there glided a second female figure, at the sight of which the first turned and fled, littering piercing shrieks as the other followed her from storey to storey.

Sick almost with terror, Graham Coulton watched the dreadful pair as they fled upstairs past the locked room to the top of the house.

It was a few minutes before he recovered his self-possession. When he did so, and searched the upper apartments, he found them totally empty.

That night, ere lying down before the fire, he carefully locked and bolted the drawing-room door; before he did more he drew the heavy settle in front of it, so that if the lock were forced no entrance could be effected without considerable noise.

For some time he lay awake, then dropped into a deep sleep, from which he was awakened suddenly by a noise as if of something scuffling stealthily behind the wainscot. He raised himself on his elbow and listened, and, to his consternation, beheld seated at the opposite side of the hearth the same woman he had seen before in his dreams, lamenting over her gold.

The fire was not quite out, and at that moment shot up a last tongue of flame. By the light, transient as it was, he saw that the figure pressed a ghostly finger to its lips, and by the turn of its head and the attitude of its body seemed to be listening.

He listened also—indeed, he was too much frightened to do aught else; more and more distinct grew the sounds which had aroused him, a stealthy rustling coming nearer and nearer—up and up it seemed, behind the wainscot.

'It is rats,' thought the young man, though, indeed, his teeth were almost chattering in his head with fear. But then in a moment ne saw what disabused him of that idea—the gleam of a candle or lamp through a crack in the panelling. He tried to rise, he strove to shout—all in vain; and, sinking down, remembered nothing more till he awoke to find the grey light of an early morning stealing through one of the shutters he had left partially unclosed.

For hours after his breakfast, which he scarcely touched, long after William had left him at mid-day, Graham Coulton, having in the morning made a long and close survey of the house, sat thinking before the fire, then, apparently having made up his mind, he put on the hat he had bought, and went out.

When he returned the evening shadows were darkening down, but the pavements were full of people going marketing, for it was Christmas Eve, and all who had money to spend seemed bent on shopping.

It was terribly dreary inside the old house that night. Through the deserted rooms Graham could feel that ghostly semblance was wandering mournfully. When he turned his back he knew she was flitting from the mirror to the fire, from the fire to the mirror; but he was not afraid of her now—he was far more afraid of another matter he had taken in hand that day.

The horror of the silent house grew and grew upon him. He could hear the beating of his own heart in the dead quietude which reigned from garret to cellar.

At last William came; but the young man said nothing to him of what was in his mind. He talked to him cheerfully and hopefully enough— wondered where his father would think he had got to, and hoped Mr Tynan might send him some Christmas pudding. Then the man said it was time for him to go, and, when Mr Coulton went downstairs to the hall- door, remarked the key was not in it.

'No,' was the answer, 'I took it out today, to oil it.'

'It wanted oiling,' agreed William, 'for it worked terribly stiff.' Having uttered which truism he departed.

Very slowly the young man retraced his way to the drawing-room, where he only paused to lock the door on the outside; then taking off his boots he went up to the top of the house, where, entering the front attic, he waited patiently in darkness and in silence.

It was a long time, or at least it seemed long to him, before he heard the same sound which had aroused him on the previous night—a stealthy rustling—then a rush of cold air—then cautious footsteps— then the quiet opening of a door below.

It did not take as long in action as it has required to tell. In a moment the young man was out on the landing and had closed a portion of the panelling on the wall which stood open; noiselessly he crept back to the attic window, unlatched it, and sprung a rattle, the sound of which echoed far and near through the deserted streets, then rushing down the stairs, he encountered a man who, darting past him, made for the landing above; but perceiving the way of escape closed, fled down again, to find Graham struggling desperately with his fellow.

'Give him the knife—come along,' he said savagely; and next instant Graham felt something like a hot iron through his shoulder, and then heard a thud, as one of the men, tripping in his rapid flight, fell from the top of the stairs to the bottom.

At the same moment there came a crash, as if the house was falling, and faint, sick, and bleeding, young Coulton lay insensible on the threshold of the room where Miss Tynan had been murdered.

When he recovered he was in the dining-room, and a doctor was examining his wound.

Near the door a policeman stiffly kept guard. The hall was full of people; all the misery and vagabondism the streets contain at that hour was crowding in to see what had happened.

Through the midst two men were being conveyed to the station-house; one, with his head dreadfully injured, on a stretcher, the other handcuffed, uttering frightful imprecations as he went.

After a time the house was cleared of the rabble, the police took possession of it, and Mr Tynan was sent for.

'What was that dreadful noise?' asked Graham feebly, now seated on the floor, with his back resting against the wall.

'I do not know. Was there a noise?' said Mr Tynan, humouring his fancy, as he thought.

'Yes, in the drawing-room, I think; the key is in my pocket.'

Still humouring the wounded lad, Mr Tynan took the key and ran upstairs.

When he unlocked the door, what a sight met his eyes! The mirror had fallen—it was lying all over the floor shivered into a thousand pieces; the console table had been borne down by its weight, and the marble slab was shattered as well. But this was not what chained his attention.

Hundreds, thousands of gold pieces were scattered about, and an aperture behind the glass contained boxes filled with securities amid deeds amid bonds, the possession of which had cost his sister her life.

* * *

'Well, Graham, and what do you want?' asked Admiral Coulton

that evening as his eldest born appeared before him, looking somewhat pale but otherwise unchanged.

'I want nothing,' was the answer, 'but to ask your forgiveness. William has told me all the story I never knew before; and, if you let me, I will try to make it up to you for the trouble you have had. I am provided for,' went on the young fellow, with a nervous laugh; 'I have made my fortune since I left you, and another man's fortune as well.'

'I think you are out of your senses,' said the Admiral shortly.

'No, sir, I have found them,' was the answer; 'and I mean to strive and make a better thing of my life than I should ever have done had I not gone to the Old House in Vauxhall Walk.'

'Vauxhall Walk! What is the lad talking about?'

'I will tell you, sir, if I may sit down,' was Graham Coulton's answer, and then he told his story.

THE LAST OF SQUIRE ENNISMORE

"Did I see it myself? No, sir; I did not see it; and my father before me did not see it; nor his father before him, and he was Phil Regan, just the same as myself. But it is true, for all that; just as true as that you are looking at the very place where the whole thing happened. My great-grandfather (and he did not die till he was ninety-eight) used to tell, many and many's the time, how he met the stranger, night after night, walking lonesome-hike about the sands where most of the wreckage came ashore."

"And the old house, then, stood behind that belt of Scotch firs?"

"Yes; and a fine house it was, too. Hearing so much talk about it when a boy, my father said, made him often feel as if he knew every room in the building, though it had all fallen to ruin before he was born. None of the family ever lived in it after the squire went away. Nobody else could be got to stop in the place. There used to be awful noises, as if something was being pitched from the top of the great staircase down in to the hall; and then there would be a sound as if a hundred people were clinking glasses and talking all together at once. And then it seemed as if barrels were rolling in the cellars; and there would be screeches, and howls, and laughing, fit to make your blood run cold. They say there is gold hid away in the cellars; but not one has ever ventured to find it. The very children won't come here to play; and when the men are plowing the field behind, nothing will make them stay in it, once the day begins to change. When the night is coming on, and the tide creeps in on the sand, more than one thinks he has seen mighty queer things on the shore."

"But what is it really they think they see? When I asked my landlord to tell me the story from beginning to end, he said he could not remember it; and, at any rate, the whole rigmarole was nonsense, put together to please strangers."

"And what is he but a stranger himself? And how should he know the doings of real quality like the Ennismores? For they were gentry, every one of them—good old stock; and as for wickedness, you might have searched Ireland through and not found their match. It is a sure thing, though, that if Riley can't tell you the story, I can; for, as I said, my own people were in it, of a manner of speaking. So, if your honour will rest yourself off your feet, on that bit of a bank, I'll set down my creel and give you the whole pedigree of how Squire Ennismore went away from Ardwinsagh."

It was a lovely day, in the early part of June; and, as the Englishman cast himself on a low ridge of sand, he looked over Ardwinsagh Bay with a feeling of ineffable content. To his left lay the Purple Headland; to his right, a long range of breakers, that went straight out into the Atlantic till they were lost from sight; in front lay the Bay of Ardwinsagh, with its bluish-green water sparkling in the summer sunlight, and here and there breaking over some sunken rock, against which the waves spent themselves in foam.

"You see how the current's set, Sir? That is what makes it dangerous for them as doesn't know the coast, to bathe here at any time, or walk when the tide is flowing. Look how the sea is creeping in now, like a race-horse at the finish. It leaves that tongue of sand bars to the last, and then, before you could look round, it has you up to the middle. That is why I made bold to speak to you; for it is not alone on the account of Squire Ennismore the bay has a bad name. But it is about him and the old house you want to hear. The last mortal being that tried to live in it, my great-grandfather said, was a creature, by name Molly Leary; and she had neither kith nor kin, and begged for her bite and sup, sheltering herself at night in a turf cabin she had built at the back of a ditch. You may be sure she

67

thought herself a made woman when the agent said, 'Yes: she might try if she could stop in the house; there was peat and bog-wood,' he told her, 'and half-a— crown a week for the winter, and a golden guinea once Easter came,' when the house was to be put in order for the family; and his wife gave Molly some warm clothes and a blanket or two; and she was well set up.

"You may be sure she didn't choose the worst room to sleep in; and for a while all went quiet, till one night she was wakened by feeling the bedstead lifted by the four corners and shaken like a carpet. It was a heavy four-post bedstead, with a solid top: and her life seemed to go out of her with the fear. If it had been a ship in a storm off the Headland, it couldn't have pitched worse and then, all of a sudden, it was dropped with such a bang as nearly drove the heart into her mouth.

"But that, she said, was nothing to the screaming and laughing, and hustling and rushing that filled the house. If a hundred people had been running hard along the passages and tumbling downstairs, they could not have made greater noise.

"Molly never was able to tell how she got clear of the place; but a man coming late home from Ballycloyne Fair found the creature crouched under the old thorn there, with very little on her—-saving your honour's presence. She had a bad fever, and talked about strange things, and never was the same woman after."

"But what was the beginning of all this? When did the house first get the name of being haunted?"

"After the old Squire went away: that was what I purposed telling you. He did not come here to live regularly till he had got well on in years. He was near seventy at the time I am talking about; but he held himself as upright as ever, and rode as hard as the youngest; and could have drunk a whole roomful under the table, and walked up to bed as unconcerned as you please at the dead of the night.

"He was a terrible man. You couldn't lay your tongue to a wickedness he had not been in the forefront of—drinking, duelling, gambling,— all manner of sins had been meat and drink to him since he was a boy almost. But at last he did something in London so bad, so beyond the beyonds, that he thought he had best come home and live among people who did not know so much about his goings on as the English. It was said that he wanted to try and stay in this world for ever; and that he had got some secret drops that kept him well and hearty. There was something wonderful queer about him, anyhow.

"He could hold foot with the youngest; and he was strong, and had a fine fresh colour in his face; and his eyes were like a hawk's; and there was not a break in his voice—and him near upon threescore and ten!

"At last and at long last it came to be the March before he was seventy—the worst March ever known in all these parts—such blowing, sheeting, snowing, had not been experienced in the memory of man; when one blusterous night some foreign vessel went to bits on the Purple Headland. They say it was an awful sound to hear the deathery that went up high above the noise of the wind; and it was as bad a sight to see the shore there strewed with corpses of all sorts and sizes, from the little cabin-boy to the grizzled seaman.

"They never knew who they were or where they came from, but some of the men had crosses, and beads, and such like, so the priest said they belonged to him, and they were all buried deeply and decently in the chapel graveyard.

"There was not much wreckage of value drifted on shore. Most of what is lost about the Head stays there; but one thing did come into the bay—a puncheon of brandy.

"The Squire claimed it; it was his right to have all that came on his land, and he owned this sea-shore from the Head to the breakers—-every foot—so, in course, he had the brandy; and there was sore illwill because he gave his men nothing, not even a glass of whiskey.

"Well, to make a long story short, that was the most wonderful liquor anybody ever tasted. The gentry came from far and near to take share, and it was cards and dice, and drinking and story-telling night after night—week in, week out. Even on Sundays, God forgive them! The officers would drive over from Ballyclone, and sit emptying tumbler after tumbler till Monday morning came, for it made beautiful punch.

"But all at once people quit coming—a word went round that the liquor was not all it ought to be. Nobody could say what ailed it, but it got about that in some way men found it did not suit them.

"For one thing, they were losing money very fast.

"They could not make head against the Squire's luck, and a hint was dropped the puncheon ought to have been towed out to sea, and sunk in fifty fathoms of water.

"It was getting to the end of April, and fine, warm weather for the time of year, when first one and then another, and then another still, began to take notice of a stranger who walked the shore alone at night. He was a dark man, the same colour as the drowned crew lying in the chapel graveyard, and had rings in his ears, and wore a strange kind of hat, and cut wonderful antics as he walked, and had an ambling sort of gait, curious to look at. Many tried to talk to him, but he only shook his head; so, as nobody could make out where he came from or what he wanted, they made sure he was the spirit of some poor wretch who was tossing about the Head, longing for a snug corner in holy ground.

"The priest went and tried to get some sense out of him.

"'Is it Christian burial you're wanting?' asked his reverence; but the creature only shook his head.

"'Is it word sent to the wives and daughters you've left orphans and widows, you'd like?' But no; it wasn't that.

"'Is it for sin committed you're doomed to walk this way? Would masses comfort ye? There's a heathen,' said his reverence; 'Did you ever hear tell of a Christian that shook his head when masses were mentioned?'

"'Perhaps he doesn't understand English, Father,' says one of the officers who was there; 'Try him with Latin.'

"No sooner said than done. The priest started off with such a string of ayes and paters that the stranger fairly took to his heels and ran.

"'He is an evil spirit,' explained the priest, when he stopped, tired out, 'and I have exorcised him.'"

"But next night my gentleman was back again, as unconcerned as ever."

'And he'll just have to stay,' said his reverence, 'For I've got lumbago in the small of my back, and pains in all my joints—never to speak of a hoarseness with standing there shouting; and I don't believe he understood a sentence I said.'

"Well, this went on for a while, and people got that frightened of the man, or appearance of a man, they would not go near the sand; till in the end, Squire Ennismore, who had always scoffed at the talk, took it into his head he would go down one night, and see into the rights of the matter."

He, maybe, was feeling lonesome, because, as I told your honour

71

before, people had left off coming to the house, and there was nobody for him to drink with.

"Out he goes, then, bold as brass; and there were a few followed him. The man came forward at sight of the Squire and took off his hat with a foreign flourish. Not to be behind in civility, the Squire lifted his."

'I have come, sir,' he said, speaking very loud, to try to make him understand, 'to know if you are looking for anything, and whether I can assist you to find it.'

"The man looked at the Squire as if he had taken the greatest liking to him, and took oft his hat again."

'Is it the vessel that was wrecked you are distressed about?'

"There came no answer, only a mournful shake of the head."

'Well, I haven't your ship, you know; it went all to bits months ago; and, as for the sailors, they are snug and sound enough in consecrated ground.'

"The man stood and looked at the Squire with a queer sort of smile on his face."

"'What do you want?' asked Mr. Ennismore in a bit of a passion. 'If anything belonging to you went down with the vessel, it's about the Head you ought to be looking for it, not here—-unless, indeed, its after the brandy you're fretting!'"

"Now, the Squire had tried him in English and French, and was now speaking a language you'd have thought nobody could understand; but, faith, it seemed natural as kissing to the stranger."

"'Oh! That's where you are from, is it?' said the Squire. 'Why couldn't you have told me so at once? I can't give you the brandy, because it mostly is drunk; but come along, and you shall have as stiff a glass of punch as ever crossed your lips.' And without more to-do off they went, as sociable as you please, jabbering together in some outlandish tongue that made moderate folks' jaws ache to hear it."

"That was the first night they conversed together, but it wasn't the last. The stranger must have been the height of good company, for the Squire never tired of him. Every evening, regularly, he came up to the house, always dressed the same, always smiling and polite, and then the Squire called for brandy and hot water, and they drank and played cards till cock-crow, talking and laughing into the small hours."

"This went on for weeks and weeks, nobody knowing where the man came from, or where he went; only two things the old housekeeper did know— that the puncheon was nearly empty, and that the Squire's flesh was wasting off him; and she felt so uneasy she went to the priest, but he could give her no manner of comfort."

"She got so concerned at last that she felt bound to listen at the dining-room door; but they always talked in that foreign gibberish, and whether it was blessing or cursing they were at she couldn't tell."

"Well, the upshot of it came one night in July—on the eve of the Squire's birthday—there wasn't a drop of spirit left in the puncheon—-no, not as much as would drown a fly. They had drunk the whole lot clean up—and the old woman stood trembling, expecting every minute to hear the bell ring for more brandy, for where was she to get more if they wanted any?"

"All at once the Squire and the stranger came out into the hall. It was a full moon, and light as day."

73

"'I'll go home with you to-night by way of a change,' says the Squire."

"'Will you so?' asked the other."

"'That I will,' answered the Squire. "'It is your own choice, you know.'"

"'Yes; it is my own choice; let us go.'"

"So they went. And the housekeeper ran up to the window on the great staircase and watched the way they took. Her niece lived there as housemaid, and she came and watched, too; and, after a while, the butler as well. They all turned their faces this way, and looked after their master walking beside the strange man along these very sands. Well, they saw them walk on, and on, and on, and on, till the water took them to their knees, and then to their waists, and then to their arm-pits, and then to their throats and their heads; but long before that the women and the butler were running out on the shore as fast as they could, shouting for help."

"Well?" said the Englishman.

"Living or dead, Squire Ennismore never came back again. Next morning, when the tides ebbed again, one walking over the sand saw the print of a cloven foot—that he tracked to the water's edge. Then everybody knew where the Squire had gone, and with whom."

"And no more search was made?"

"Where would have been the use searching?"

"Not much, I suppose. It's a strange story, anyhow."

"But true, your honour—every word of it."

"Oh! I have no doubt of that," was the satisfactory reply.

THE END

www.ingramcontent.com/pod-product-compliance
Lightning Source LLC
Chambersburg PA
CBHW032217120625
28169CB00003B/103